13

Paddington's Magical Christmas

Michael Bond
Illustrated by David McKee

COLLINS

William Collins Sons & Co Ltd
London · Glasgow · Sydney · Auckland
Toronto · Johannesburg

First published 1988
© text Michael Bond 1988
© illustrations William Collins Sons & Co Ltd and David McKee 1988

British Library Cataloguing in Publication Data

Bond, Michael, 1926-   Paddington's magical Christmas.
I. Title   II. McKee, David, 1935- 823'.914[J]

ISBN 0 00 181180-0

Printed and bound in Spain
Cronion S.A.

One day, not long before Christmas, Paddington was busy doing his accounts when he heard Mrs Bird singing, which was most unusual.

Then, as he listened to the words, he nearly fell off his chair with surprise. It seemed her true love had sent her a present of a partridge in a pear tree.

As it happened, Paddington was having trouble deciding what to buy the Brown family for Christmas and he wished he had thought of it himself.

He hurried out into the garden, but to his disappointment he couldn't see a pear tree anywhere, let alone one with a partridge in it.

He gazed hopefully at Mr Brown's apple tree, but, apart from a few sparrows and a robin redbreast, the branches were bare.

Paddington made his way back indoors, and no sooner was he inside than he heard Mrs Brown singing that *her* true love had sent four calling birds, three French hens, and two turtle doves, not to mention another partridge in a pear tree.

Paddington could hardly believe his ears and he hurried back outside as fast as he could go.

But once again he was too late. Even the sparrows and the robin redbreast had flown away and all that was left was one fat old pigeon sitting on the lawn.

All the same, Paddington decided to keep his eyes and ears open. Clearly there was something going on.

Sure enough, no sooner had he settled down than it was Judy's turn to break into song.

This time she announced that as well as Mrs Brown getting four calling birds, three French hens, two turtle doves and a partridge in a pear tree, *she* had been given five gold rings.

Paddington decided that the Browns must have a very rich friend indeed if he could afford so many presents. It made his own list look very small. He couldn't afford much more than a set of plastic rings, let alone five gold ones.

Over the next few days the mystery deepened.
Seven swans a-swimming arrived, and disappeared again before Paddington had a chance to see them. He even tried looking in the oven, but Mrs Bird drove him out of the kitchen with her feather duster.

Eight maids a-milking came and went, although Paddington did find a note on the front doorstep asking for "two extra pints, please."

He began to wonder if he ought to ring for the police, but no one else seemed to be in the slightest bit worried.

When Paddington heard what Mrs Bird sang next – nine ladies dancing – he decided that perhaps she had ordered the extra milk in case they got thirsty. He searched the house from top to bottom, but there was no sign of anybody. And then, just as he was about to come downstairs, he heard Jonathan singing. It seemed that he had been sent no less than ten lords a-leaping.

Paddington decided to go and see his friend, Mr Gruber, who kept an antique shop in the Portobello Road. Apart from all the antiques, Mr Gruber also had piles of books about every subject under the sun, and Paddington felt sure he would be able to explain the mystery.

As soon as Paddington arrived, Mr Gruber made some cocoa and they settled down on the horsehair sofa at the back of his shop.

"Tell me, Mr Brown," he said. "What is the problem? I can see you are very worried about something."

"Mrs Bird has fallen in love with a very rich man who has lots of servants and keeps birds," said Paddington. "He's sent all sorts of Christmas presents, but as fast as they arrive, they disappear."

Mr Gruber listened carefully as Paddington told him the story.

"I think, Mr Brown," he said at last, "that if you were to go back to number thirty-two Windsor Gardens you would probably find he's sent eleven pipers piping as well."

Paddington gazed at Mr Gruber in astonishment. He was used to his friend knowing the answers to his problems, but this was the fastest ever.

He finished his cocoa as quickly as possible and he was about to leave when, to his surprise, Mr Gruber began pulling the blind down over his shop door.

"You see, Mr Brown," he explained, "they haven't really been getting presents. They have all been joining in singing a Christmas carol. But you have given me an idea for *your* present. We shall have to hurry, though. It's Christmas Eve and a lot of the shops will be closing early."

With Paddington trying to keep up with him, Mr Gruber led the way along the Portobello Road, and as they weaved their way through the stalls lining the street he explained what he had in mind.

Paddington grew more and more excited as he listened.

"I don't think I shall sleep very much tonight, Mr Gruber," he said.

"Just leave it to me," said Mr Gruber. "I think between us, and with the help of some of our friends in the market, we shall be able to give everyone a Christmas to remember."

Mr Gruber was as good as his word, and on Christmas morning, soon after breakfast, a very strange procession began making its way from the market towards number thirty-two Windsor Gardens.

On the twelfth day of Christmas my true love sent to me
Twelve drummers drumming . . .

Eleven pipers piping . . .

Ten lords a-leaping . . .

Nine ladies dancing . . .

Eight maids a-milking . . .

Seven swans a-swimming . . .

Six geese a-laying . . .

Five gold rings . . .

Four calling birds . . .

Three French hens . . .

Two turtle doves . . .

And a partridge in a pear tree . . .

"If you ask me," said Mrs Bird, as she invited everyone in for hot mince pies fresh from the oven, "that's the nicest start to a Christmas Day anyone could possibly wish for. But then," she added, amid general agreement, "with a bear like Paddington about the house, life is always full of lovely surprises."

3513